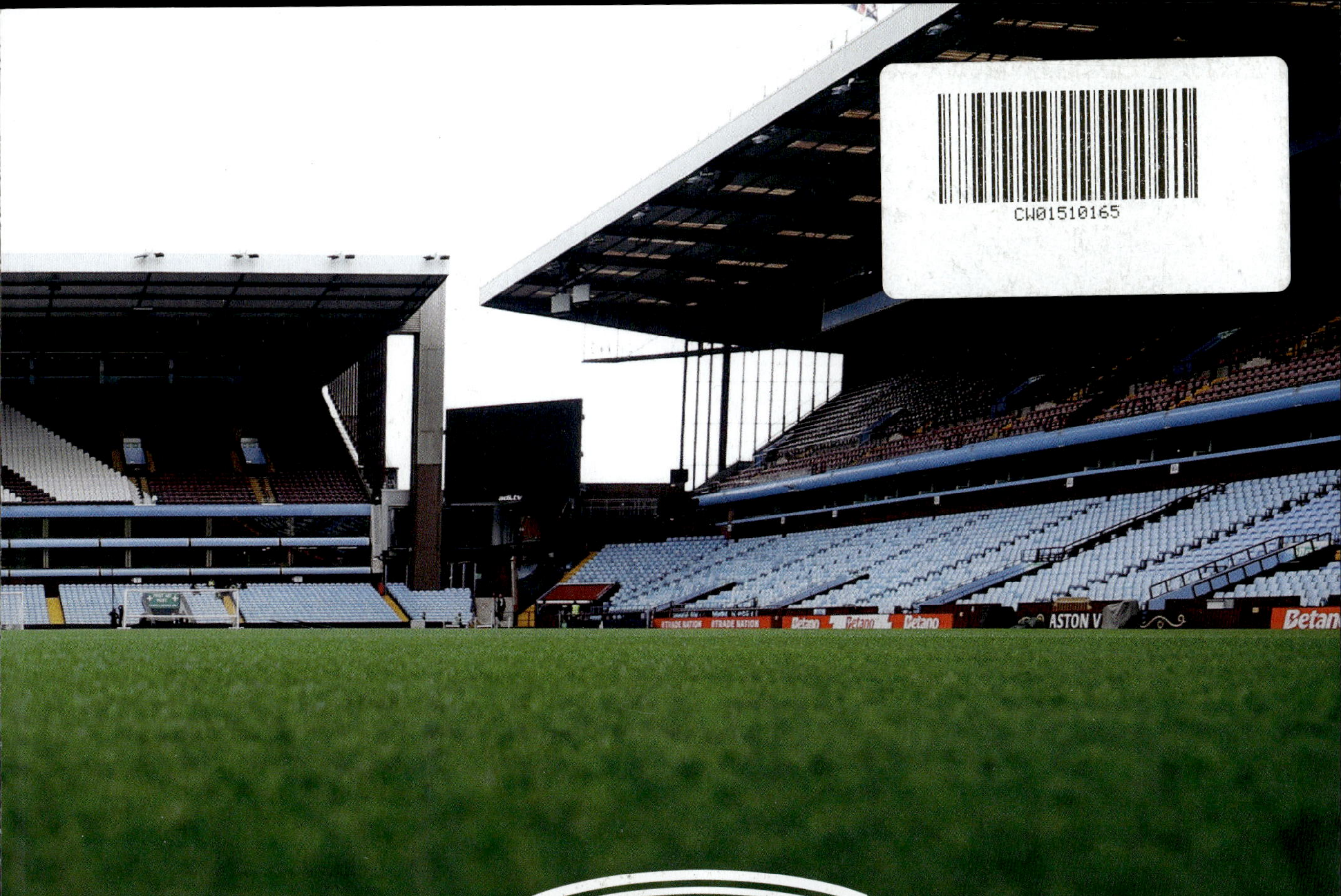

THE OFFICIAL

ASTON VILLA

ANNUAL 2025

Compiled by Rob Bishop and Dan Brawn,
with special thanks to Gayner Monkton.

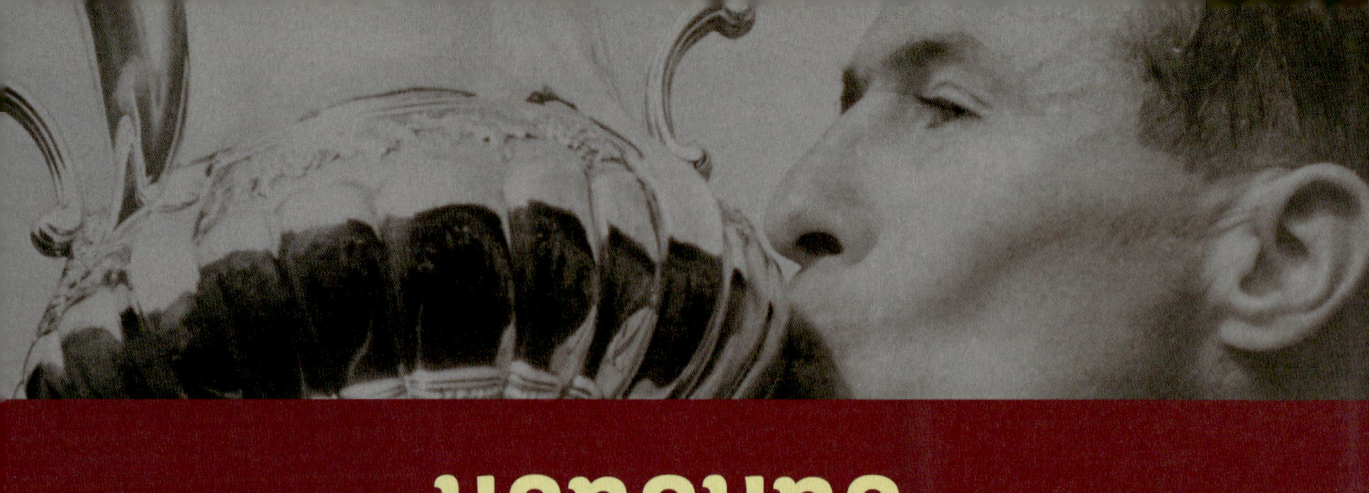

HONOURS

1 EUROPEAN CUP
Winners: 1981-82

1 EUROPEAN SUPER CUP
Winners: 1982-83

1 INTERTOTO CUP
Winners: 2001

World Club Championships
Runners-up: 1982

7 FOOTBALL LEAGUE /
PREMIER LEAGUE
Champions: 1893-94,
1895-96, 1896-97, 1898-
99, 1899-1900, 1909-10,
1980-81

Runners-up: 1888-89, 1902-03, 1907-08,
1910-11, 1912-13, 1913-14, 1930-31,
1932-33,1989-90

Premier League **Runners-up**: 1992-93

1 CHAMPIONSHIP/
DIVISION ONE
Play-off Winners: 2019

2 DIVISION TWO
Champions: 1937-38,
1959-60

1 DIVISION THREE
Champions: 1971-72

7 FA CUP
Winners: 1887, 1895, 1897,
1905, 1913, 1920, 1957

Runners-up: 1892, 1924, 2000, 2015

5 LEAGUE CUP
Winners: 1961, 1975, 1977,
1994, 1996

Runners-up: 1963, 1971, 2010, 2020

1 CHARITY SHIELD
Joint Winners: 1981

4 FA YOUTH CUP
Winners: 1972, 1980,
2002, 2021

Runners-up: 2004, 2010

CONTENTS

New Signings	6
We Are Champions League	10
Safe As Houses	13
Friendly Globetrotters!	14
24/25 Squad Profiles	16
Home, Sweet Home	23
Do You Know Emi Martinez?	25
Which Is My Shirt?	26
Fact Or Fib?	27
23/24 Season Review	29
Back On The Euro Trail	40
Off The Mark	42
Euro Rivals Quiz	44
Are You An AV Student?	45
The Numbers Game	46
Doing Your Homework	49
Kosta Kilo!	50
Which Club Did I Sign From?	51
Spot The Difference	53
A Century And A Half Of Memories	54
Become Part Of The Villa	56
Spot The Ball	58
The Debut Line-Up!	59
Quiz Answers	60

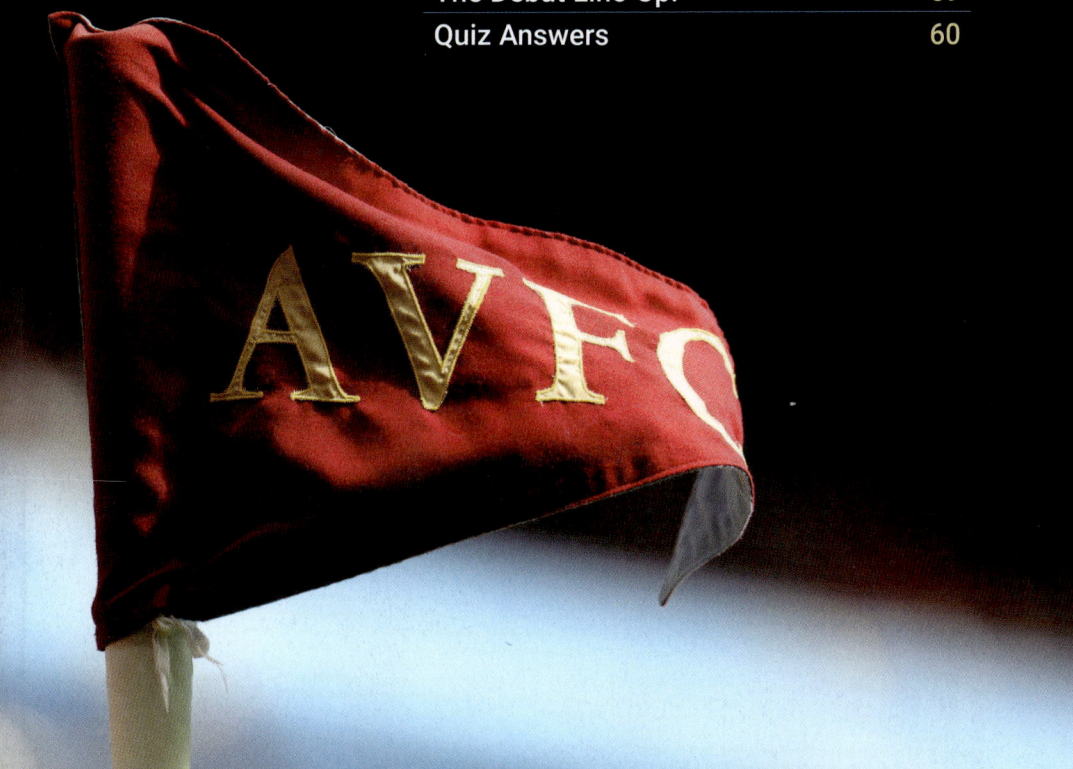

NEW SIGNINGS

LET'S HEAR IT FOR THE FANS!

One thing was missing the last time Ross Barkley signed for Villa – spectators.

When the England international arrived on loan from Chelsea at the start of the 2020-21 season, Britain was still in the grip of the Covid-19 pandemic, with no supporters allowed.

"The last time I was here I didn't play in front of the fans, and I missed that," he said. "It's different now. The atmosphere is great when Villa Park is full."

After starting his career with his hometown club Everton, Barkley won both the FA Cup and UEFA Europa League with Chelsea before linking up with Villa. He has since played for French club Nice and Luton Town.

THE WAITING GAME...

Ian Maatsen had to be patient after joining Villa from Chelsea at the end of June.

The transfer was completed while the Dutch left-back had other things on his mind – he was a member of the Netherlands squad for the 2024 European Championships in Germany.

It meant he was unable to visit the Bodymoor Heath until almost a month later, beginning pre-season training later than most of his new team-mates because of his involvement in the Euros.

"I couldn't wait to get started," he said. "I saw the boys in training on their social media accounts and I just wanted to get to know them.

"It's a challenge for me to come here and show people I am capable of performing at the highest level. I'm an exciting player and I love to play football. I enjoy tackles and I like to get the crowd going."

Maatsen was also excited at the prospect of playing in the Champions League, although that experience is nothing new to him.

He was on loan to Borussia Dortmund for the second half of last season and helped the German giants to the final, which they narrowly lost 2-0 to Real Madrid at Wembley. He was also named in the competition's team of the season.

WELCOME HOME!

Jaden Philogene is hoping his Villa career will take off at the second time of asking after returning for a second spell in claret and blue.

After a successful season with Hull City, the winger was more than happy when Unai Emery wanted to re-sign him for Villa.

"It's like I am back at home," he said. "Unai spoke to me and we had a good conversation. He said I did well in pre-season last year and that I'm going to get chances this time. It depends on how I play!

"It's the latest chapter of my Villa journey. Hopefully I can get game time and do it in front of the fans."

Jaden made his Villa debut in a 2-1 win at Tottenham in May 2021 and had loan spells with Cardiff City and Stoke City before moving to Hull. He scored 12 Championship goals during his season with the Tigers.

THE ITALIAN JOB

Did you hear about the Englishman and the Argentinian youngsters who joined Villa on the same day – from an Italian club?

It sounds unlikely but it happened during the summer when winger Samuel Iling-Junior and defensive midfielder Enzo Barrenechea were signed from Juventus.

It's a dream move for Barrenechea, who gained valuable experience in Serie A while on loan at Frosinone last season.

"I want to contribute, and help my team-mates," he said. "I like to work hard. This is a big club with a good structure and top-level facilities, and they are playing in one of the best leagues in the world."

Iling-Junior, who was born in London and was a youth player at Chelsea before moving to Juventus. He is equally delighted at joining Villa and hopes to make an impression on the claret-and-blue faithful when the opportunity arises.

"I want to play with a smile on my face and enjoy the game," he said. "I want to excite the fans as much as possible and create a bond with them."

Both players were both loaned out at the start of the season, Iling-Junior returning to Italy to link up with Bologna while Barrenechea joined Spanish club Valencia.

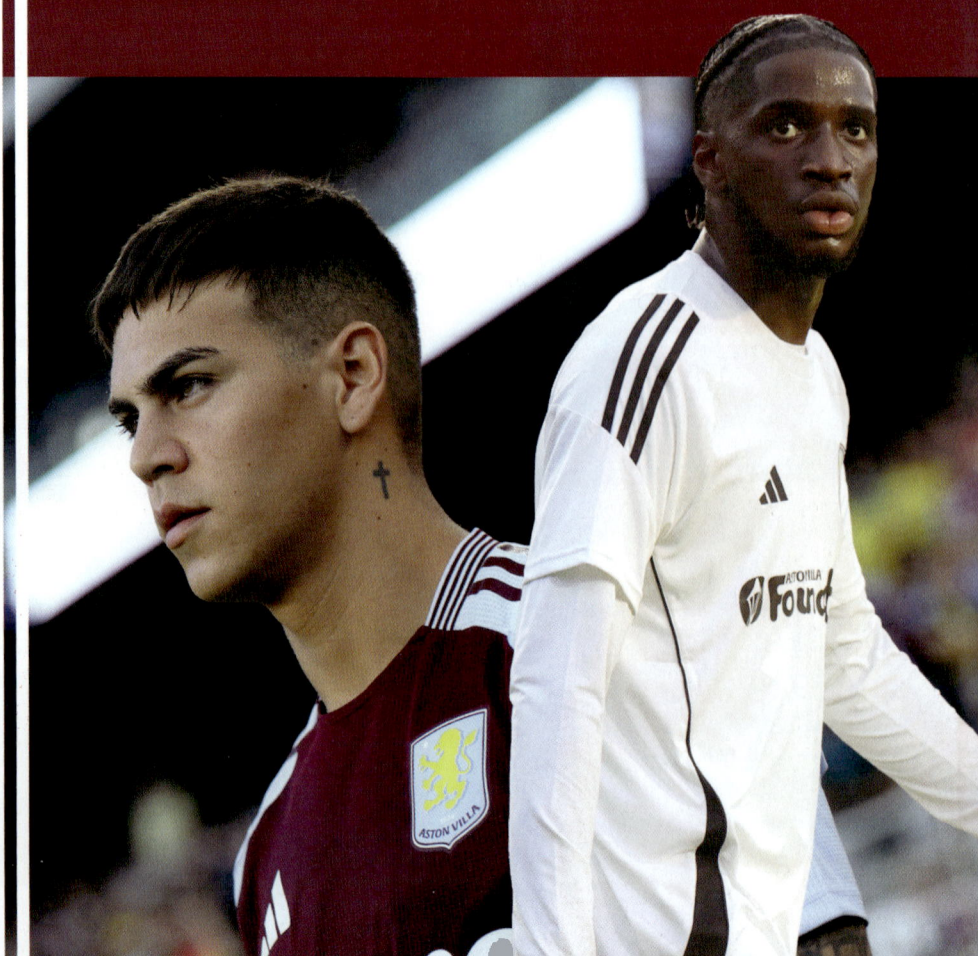

FOR CLUB AND COUNTRY

Amadou Onana had plenty of inside information when he decided to join Villa from Everton – his Belgium international team-mate Youri Tielemans had already been a Villan for 12 months.

"Youri played a big part in bringing me here," said the towering midfielder.

"He told me lots of good stuff about the club. He is someone I'm used to playing alongside so I'm enjoying training with him on a daily basis. He also has the experience to guide me through the process of settling into the club.

"It's amazing to be here. There's a healthy atmosphere to grow as a player – and as a man. The team played very attractive football last season, with loads of goals.

"We also have a manager who is one of the best in the business. I think he can take my game to the next level."

Onana arrived at Villa Park after making 63 Premier League appearances for Everton after joining them from French club Lille OSC. As a result, he was aware of what a special place Villa Park is, even before his transfer.

"It's a great stadium with a great atmosphere," he said. "And the fans are amazing!"

GOING DUTCH...

Lamare Bogarde wasn't a new signing, but it must have felt like it. The Dutch defender signed a new contract in August and finally made his Premier League debut – four years after joining Villa from Feyenoord.

Bogarde's only previous senior game was an FA Cup tie against Liverpool in January 2021, when Villa were forced to field a team of youth players because of a Covid-19 outbreak among the first-team squad.

But when Matty Cash and Diego Carlos were both injured, he played at right-back in a 2-1 win at Leicester City, earning rich praise from Unai Emery.

"When we use young players, it's because they have potential," said the manager. "They must be ready, knowing our style, ideas and demands.

"Bogarde had some good games in pre-season. After the injuries to Cash and Carlos, we needed a different option. He has quality and did well."

Only six years ago, Villa were playing in the EFL Championship – now they are competing in the UEFA Champions League!

From English football's second tier to Europe's most prestigious club competition is an amazing feat – particularly as Villa were in danger when Unai Emery was appointed head coach.

Under Unai's guidance, the boys in claret and blue rocketed up the Premier League table to finish seventh and qualify for the Europa Conference League.

And that was followed by fourth place last season with the help of 19 goals from Ollie Watkins, who became the club's highest scorer in a Premier League season.

WE ARE CHAM

PIONS LEAGUE!

The last time we played in UEFA's top tournament was in the early 1980s, when it was still known as the European Cup.

After beating Valur (Iceland), Dynamo Berlin (East Germany), Dynamo Kiev (USSR) and Anderlecht (Belgium), Villa beat West German giants Bayern Munich 1-0 in the final in Rotterdam.

They were very much the underdogs and their cause wasn't helped when goalkeeper Jimmy Rimmer was injured after just nine minutes. But the inexperienced Nigel Spink took over between the posts and made a succession of fine saves before Peter Withe scored the winning goal in the 67th minute.

Around 12,000 Villa supporters celebrated in the Netherlands, while ITV viewers were treated to Brian Moore's commentary, which has become part of claret and blue folklore: "It must be – and it is! Peter Withe!"

The kit Villa wore in the final – white shirts with a claret pinstripe – is one of the most popular replica shirts in football history.

EZRI KONSA

ASTON VILLA
1874

SAFE AS HOUSES

LITTLE HOUSE, CHELTENHAM

Brian Little was one of the finest players in Villa's history. He made his debut when they were in the Third Division and helped the club back to the top flight in 1975, when he also played in the League Cup final victory over Norwich City. He scored the winner in the 1977 final against Everton and played 302 games, scoring 82 goals.

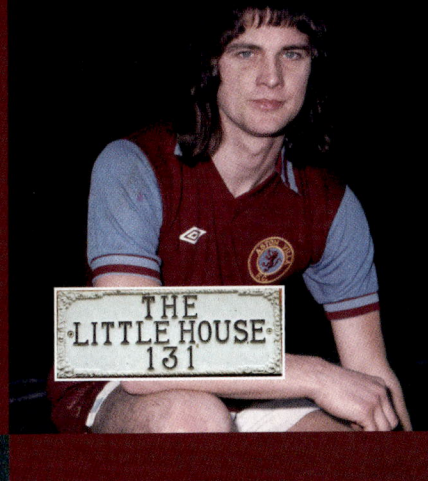

MOUNTFIELD HOUSE, KINGSWINFORD

Derek Mountfield made 120 Villa appearances and scored 17 goals after signing from Everton in 1988. His most successful season in claret and blue was 1989-90, when he formed a formidable central defensive trio with Paul McGrath and Kent Nielsen as Villa finished runners-up to Liverpool. He joined Wolves early in 1992.

WESLEY HOUSE, BUDE, CORNWALL

Along with Douglas Luiz, striker **Wesley Moraes** was one of the first Brazilian players to join Villa when he signed from Belgian club Bruges in 2019. He scored five goals before being seriously injured at Burnley on New Year's Day 2020 and was unable to re-establish a regular place.

It's good to see that several buildings – both residential and business premises – carry the names of former Villa players. Here are a few we spotted on our travels...

ASHLEY HOUSE, FOWEY, CORNWALL

We're cheating a little here, by using a Christian name rather than a surname, but this one is perfect for **Ashley Young**. The winger joined Villa from Watford in 2007 and subsequently played for Manchester United and Inter Milan before returning in 2021 for two more seasons in claret and blue.

FRIENDLY

There was a time when pre-season match action amounted to no more than a game between the first team and the reserves on the Saturday before the new campaign got underway.

Not any longer! Villa's preparations for 2023-24 involved seven warm-up games in four different countries. The schedule got underway close to home, a 3-0 win against Walsall at Bescot, before the team flew to Slovakia, where they beat Spartak Trnava by the same scoreline.

Villa's three games in the United States didn't go so well, with defeats at the hands of Columbus Crew, Germans RB Leipzig in New Jersey and Mexican club America in Chicago.

But the team bounced back with a 3-2 "home" success against Spain's Athletic Bilbao at Walsall before signing off with a 2-0 defeat to Borussia Dortmund in Germany, where the attendance was a staggering 81,365!

GLOBETROTTERS!

THE 24/25 SQUAD

GK

EMILIANO
MARTINEZ

 MAR DEL PLATA,
ARGENTINA

 02.09.1992

 SEPTEMBER 2020
ARSENAL

GK

JOE
GAUCI

 ADELAIDE,
AUSTRALIA

 04.07.2000

 JANUARY 2024
ADELAIDE UNITED

GK

ROBIN
OLSEN

 MALMO,
SWEDEN

 08.01.1990

 JUNE 2022
ROMA

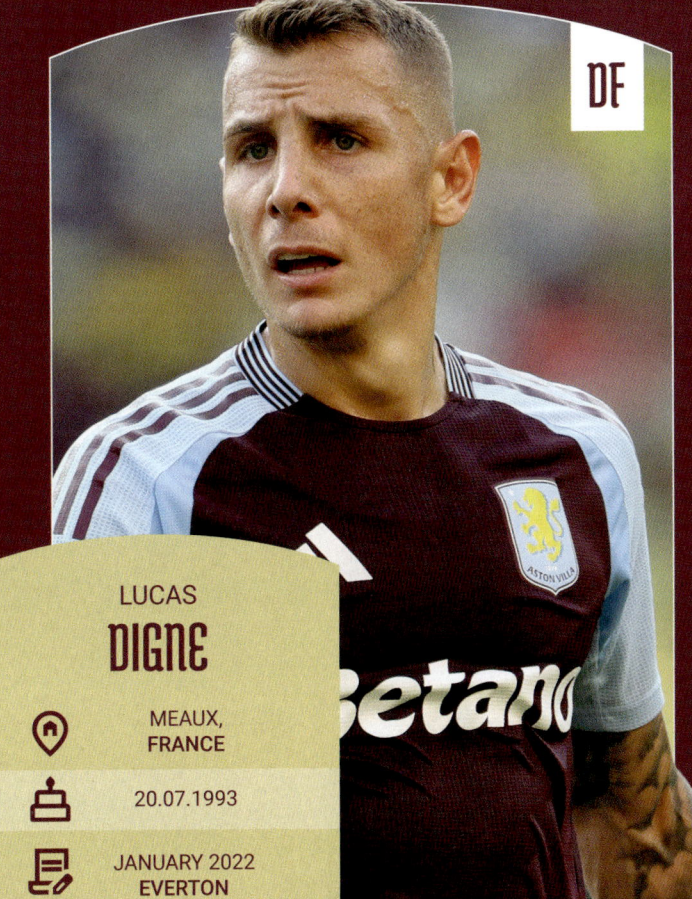

DF

LUCAS
DIGNE

 MEAUX,
FRANCE

 20.07.1993

 JANUARY 2022
EVERTON

DF

KOSTA
NEDELJKOVIC

 SMEDEREVO
SERBIA

 12.12.2005

 JANUARY 2024
RED STAR BELGRADE

DF

ALEX
MORENO

 BARCELONA, SPAIN

 08.06.1993

 JANUARY 2023
REAL BETIS

DF

TYRONE
MINGS

 BATH, ENGLAND

 13.03.1993

JULY 2019
BOURNEMOUTH

DF

EZRI
KONSA

 NEWHAM, ENGLAND

 23.10.1997

 JULY 2019
BRENTFORD

DF

DIEGO
CARLOS

SAO PAULO, BRAZIL

15.03.1993

MAY 2022
SEVILLA

DF

IAN
MAATSEN

 VLAARDINGEN, NETHERLANDS

 10.03.2002

 JUNE 2024
CHELSEA

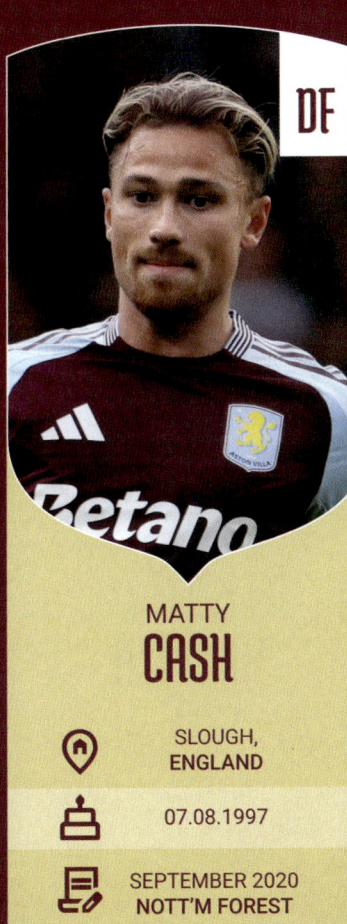

DF

MATTY
CASH

SLOUGH,
ENGLAND

07.08.1997

SEPTEMBER 2020
NOTT'M FOREST

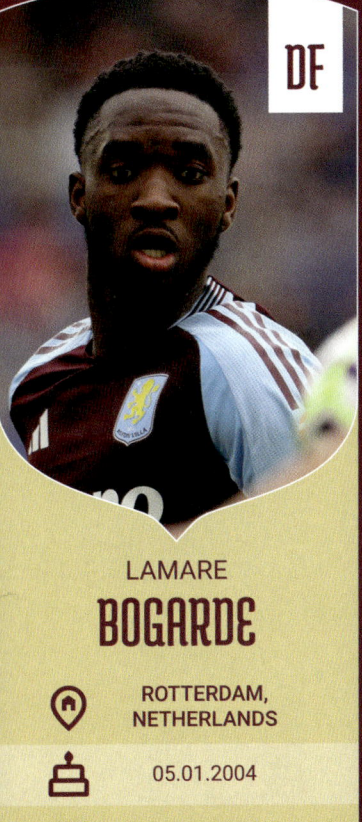

DF

LAMARE
BOGARDE

ROTTERDAM,
NETHERLANDS

05.01.2004

SEPTEMBER 2020
FEYENOORD

MF

SAMUEL
ILING-JUNIOR

LONDON,
ENGLAND

04.10.2003

JULY 2024
JUVENTUS

MF

JOHN
McGINN

GLASGOW,
SCOTLAND

18.10.1994

AUGUST 2018
HIBERNIAN

19

MF

ENZO
BARRENECHEA

 VILLA MARIA,
ARGENTINA

 22.05.2001

 JULY 2024
JUVENTUS

MF

AMADOU
ONANA

 DAKAR,
SENEGAL

 16.08.2001

JULY 2024
EVERTON

MF

BOUBACAR
KAMARA

 MARSEILLE,
FRANCE

 23.11.1999

 MAY 2022
MARSEILLE

MF

JACOB
RAMSEY

 BIRMINGHAM,
ENGLAND

 28.05.2001

 ACADEMY
GRADUATE

MF

ROSS
BARKLEY

 LIVERPOOL,
ENGLAND

 05.12.1993

 JULY 2024
LUTON TOWN

MF

LEANDER
DENDONCKER

 PASSENDALE,
BELGIUM

 15.04.95

 SEPTEMBER 2022
WOLVES

MF

EMILIANO
BUENDIA

 MAR DEL PLATA,
ARGENTINA

 25.12.1996

 JULY 2021
NORWICH CITY

MF

LEON
BAILEY

 KINGSTON,
JAMAICA

 09.08.1997

 AUGUST 2022
B. LEVERKUSEN

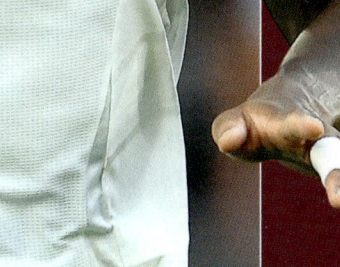

FW

JHON
DURAN

 MEDELLIN,
COLOMBIA

 13.12.2003

 JANUARY 2023
CHICAGO FIRE

21

FW

MORGAN
ROGERS

 HALESOWEN,
ENGLAND

 26.07.2002

FEBRUARY 2024
MIDDLESBROUGH

FW

LEWIS
DOBBIN

 STOKE-ON-TRENT,
ENGLAND

 03.01.2003

 JUNE 2024
EVERTON

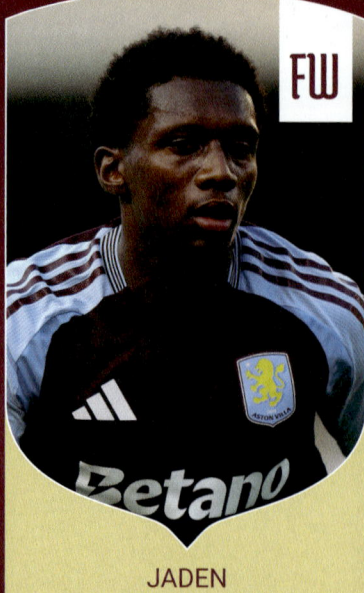

FW

JADEN
PHILOGENE

 LONDON,
ENGLAND

 08.02.2002

 JULY 2024
HULL CITY

OLLIE
WATKINS

TORQUAY,
ENGLAND

30.12.1995

SEPTEMBER 2020
BRENTFORD

HOME, SWEET HOME...

It wouldn't be surprising if Morgan Rogers' favourite school subject was Geography. During his short career, he has played for clubs all over the country.

A graduate of West Brom's academy, the attacking midfielder was snapped up by Manchester City in 2019 and subsequently had spells on loan at Lincoln

away on your own. You're like, 'I wish I was back home', so it's a perfect opportunity for me, being back home playing for such a big club."

Rogers describes himself as a "free spirit" on the pitch, adding: "I want to get fans off their seats." "It's a bit surreal at times, coming to the training ground every day," Rogers told Sky

integrate in the dressing room, full of players he already knew well from his academy days.

He has bags of talent and he showed glimpses of real quality in his 60-minute showing against Luton.

> "There's nothing better than playing football at home, around your family, being closer to them and friends,"

City, Bournemouth and Blackpool, before signing for Middlesbrough.

Even so, he leapt at the chance of playing his football at Villa Park, which is just eight miles from his home town of Halesowen.

"There's nothing better than playing football at home, around your family, being closer to them and friends," he said. "Nothing really beats it.

"Obviously I have been away for a while and you take it for granted a bit when you're

Sports. "It still feels a bit weird that I'm here actually and that I am a Villa player. I'm just so happy and grateful for the opportunity."

Rogers has taken no time to settle at Villa and

PAU TORRES

DO YOU KNOW
EMI MARTINEZ?

From which club did Emi sign for Villa?

☐ A. Arsenal

☐ B. River Plate

☐ C. Chelsea

Which country did he help to World Cup glory in 2022?

☐ A. Brazil

☐ B. Uruguay

☐ C. Argentina

Against which club did Emi make his Villa debut?

☐ A. Man United

☐ B. Sheff United

☐ C. Tottenham

Against which team did he save two penalties in a Europa Conference League match last season?

☐ A. AZ Alkmaar

☐ B. Olympiacos

☐ C. Lille OSC

Where was he born?

☐ A. Buenos Aires

☐ B. Mar Del Plata

☐ C. Mendoza

Answers on page 60.

WHICH IS MY SHIRT?

Villa's players will be confused when they go into the dressing room – the names on their shirts have been jumbled up! Can you solve these anagrams to reveal the correct names?

Answers on page 60.

STORER 1

MEET SNAIL 2

NO MORE 3

AA MARK 4

KRAB YEL 5

NO ASK 6

RAM IT ZEN 7

SINK TAW 8

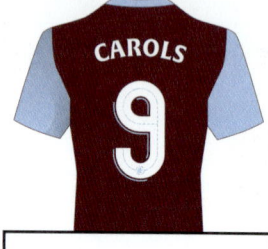
CAROLS 9

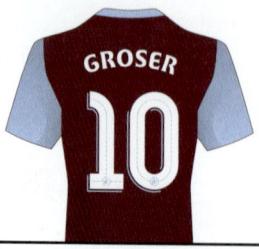
GROSER 10

MY EARS 11

DARN U 12

FACT OR FIB?

How much do you know about Villa? Some of these statements are factual, others are incorrect. See if you can get ten out of ten! To get you started, No.1 is a **FACT** – Ollie Watkins was Villa's leading scorer last season.

Answers on page 60.

1. Ollie Watkins was Villa's leading scorer in 2023-24.

✓ TRUE ☐ FALSE

4. Matty Cash netted a late goal against Lille, in the Europa Conference League to send the game to penalties.

☐ TRUE ☐ FALSE

8. The European Conference League tie against Hibernian was the first time the club had faced Scottish opposition in UEFA competitions.

☐ TRUE ☐ FALSE

2. Watkins became the first player to score two Premier League hat-tricks for the club when he netted three goals against Brighton.

☐ TRUE ☐ FALSE

5. The home leg of the ECL quarter-final against Lille OSC was the club's 100th game in European competitions.

☐ TRUE ☐ FALSE

6. John McGinn provided the team's most goal assists.

☐ TRUE ☐ FALSE

9. Villa qualified for the UEFA Champions League for the first time.

☐ TRUE ☐ FALSE

3. Youri Tielemans joined Villa from Leeds United.

☐ TRUE ☐ FALSE

7. Villa's fourth-place finish was their highest in the Premier League.

☐ TRUE ☐ FALSE

10. Hollywood star Tom Cruise was a guest at the final home game against Liverpool.

☐ TRUE ☐ FALSE

YOURI TIELEMANS

ASTON VILLA 1874

SEASON REVIEW

2023/24

AUGUST

Not the start we wanted! After remaining unbeaten in pre-season games, Villa crash to 5-1 opening day defeat at Newcastle United, the only consolation being provided by a Moussa Diaby goal on his debut. To add to the misery, Tyrone Mings suffers a knee injury which requires an operation.

Unai Emery's men bounce back with an emphatic 4-0 home win against Everton. John McGinn opens the scoring, Douglas Luiz converts a penalty and there are second half goals for Leon Bailey and substitute Jhon Duran – his first for the club.

Full-back Matty Cash is the unlikely hero in a 3-1 success against Burnley at Turf Moor, where Diaby makes sure of maximum points after the home side reduce the deficit.

12th	NEWCASTLE UNITED (A)	1-5	*Diaby*
20th	EVERTON (H)	4-0	*McGinn, Luiz (pen), Bailey, Duran*
27th	BURNLEY (A)	3-1	*Cash 2, Diaby*

SEPTEMBER

Having scored three goals in the previous two games, Matty Cash is on target again at Anfield – this time at the wrong end! The full-back's own goal helps Liverpool to a 3-0 success.

There are also concerns in the following match when Villa trail Crystal Palace with just over three minutes of normal time remaining. But Jhon Duran hits a spectacular equaliser, and in stoppage time Douglas Luiz converts a penalty and Leon Bailey finds the net to complete a 3-1 victory.

Ollie Watkins scores his first league goal of the season to secure three points against Chelsea at Stamford Bridge, and then hits a hat-trick in a 6-1 romp against Brighton & Hove Albion.

3rd	LIVERPOOL (A)	0-3	
16th	CRYSTAL PALACE (H)	3-1	*Duran, Luiz (pen), Bailey*
24th	CHELSEA (A)	1-0	*Watkins*
27th	EVERTON (LC) (H)	1-2	*Kamara*
30th	BRIGHTON & HA (H)	6-1	*Watkins 3, Estupinan og, Ramsey, Luiz*

OCTOBER

Pau Torres scores his first goal for the club in a 1-1 draw against Wolves at Molineux, the central defender equalising from close range just two minutes after Hee Chan Hwang puts the home side ahead.

When the Premier League resumes after the international break, Unai Emery's men turn on the style with a 4-1 home win against West Ham. Douglas Luiz opens the scoring with a low shot before increasing the lead from the penalty spot. Although the Hammers reduce the deficit, goals from Ollie Watkins and substitute Leon Bailey complete an emphatic win.

Premier League new boys Luton Town are then beaten 3-1 at Villa Park. John McGinn's low angled drive opens the scoring before Moussa Diaby grabs a second and then forces Tom Lockyer into an own goal.

8th	WOLVES (A)	1-1	*Torres*
22nd	WEST HAM UNITED (H)	4-1	*Luiz 2 (1 pen), Watkins, Bailey*
29th	LUTON TOWN (H)	3-1	*McGinn, Diaby, Lockyer (og)*

NOVEMBER

After six Premier League matches without defeat, there's a big disappointment at the City Ground – a 2-0 defeat to Nottingham Forest despite Villa enjoying 73 percent possession. But they bounce back with a 3-1 home win over Fulham – a result which equals the club's post-war record of 13 consecutive home wins in the top flight.

An own goal puts Villa ahead before John McGinn doubles the lead just before half-time with an unstoppable shot. Ollie Watkins adds number 3 before Raul Jiminez reduces the deficit.

Even more impressive is a 2-1 win at Tottenham, which lifts Villa to fourth in the table. A powerful Pau Torres header and a well-worked Watkins goal secure maximum points after the home side take an early lead.

5th	NOTTINGHAM FOREST(A)	0-2	
12th	FULHAM (H)	3-1	*Robinson (og) McGinn, Watkins*
25th	TOTTENHAM HOTSPUR (A)	2-1	*Torres, Watkins*

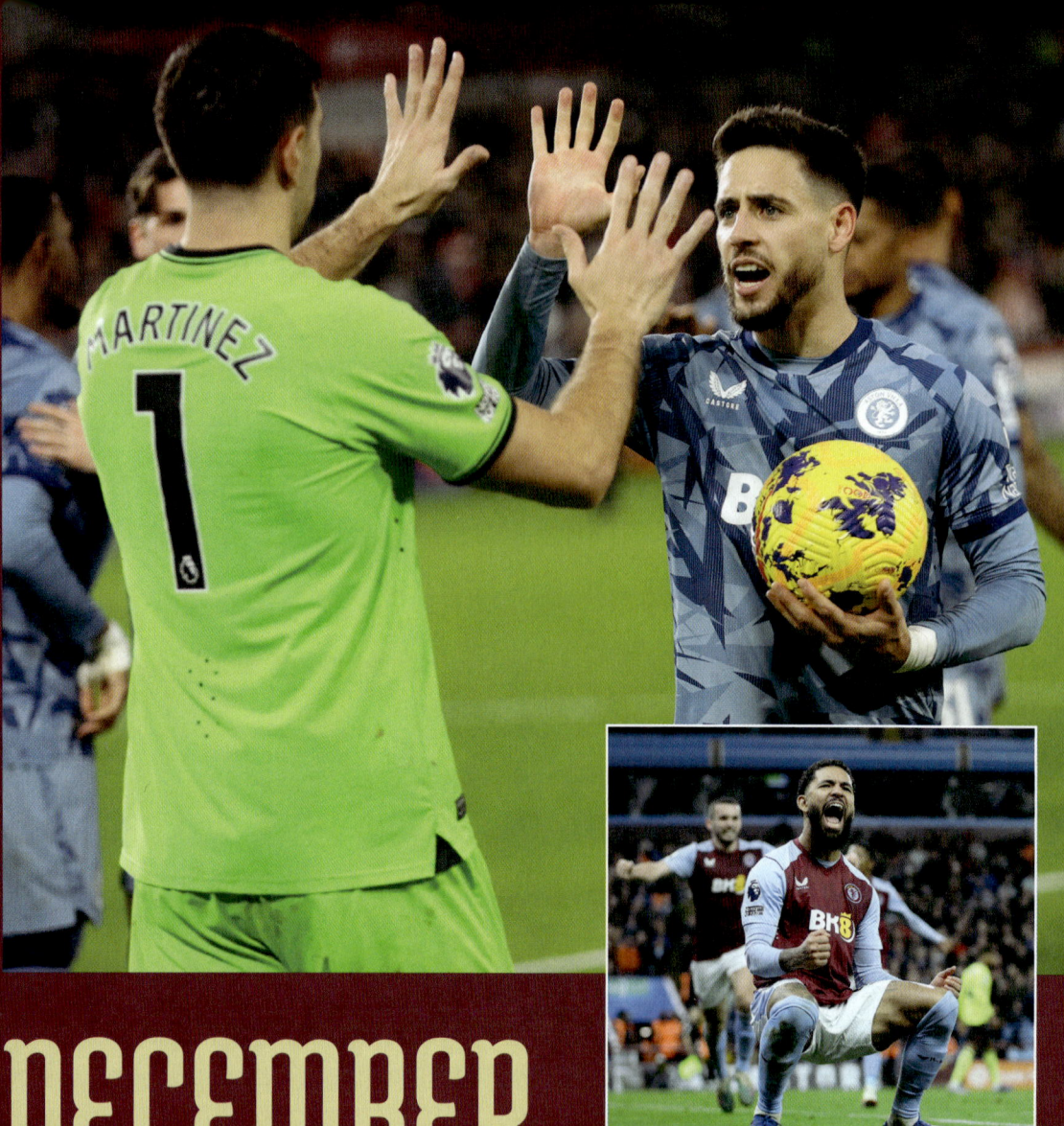

DECEMBER

After a 2-2 draw at Bournemouth, where a late Ollie Watkins header rescues a point, Villa produce a performance rated by many as their best for years to beat champions Manchester City 1-0. Leon Bailey secures all three points with a deflected shot.

Three days later, John McGinn's early goal against leaders Arsenal extends Villa's sequence of home league wins to a club record 15, while second-half goals from Alex Moreno and Ollie Watkins clinch a 2-1 success at Brentford.

The run of home wins ends with a 1-1 draw against Sheffield United, Nicolo Zaniolo scoring his first Premier League goal in stoppage time.

Despite leading Manchester United 2-0 at half-time, Villa lose 3-2 at Old Trafford before ending 2023 with victory over Burnley.

3rd	BOURNEMOUTH (A)	2-2	Bailey, Watkins
6th	MANCHESTER CITY (H)	1-0	Bailey
9th	ARSENAL (H)	1-0	McGinn
17th	BRENTFORD (A)	2-1	Moreno, Watkins
22nd	SHEFFIELD UNITED (H)	1-1	Zaniolo
26th	MANCHESTER UNITED (A)	2-3	McGinn, Dendoncker
30th	BURNLEY (H)	3-2	Bailey, Diaby, Luiz (pen)

JANUARY

The FA Cup hasn't been kind to Villa in recent years. But in the opening game of 2024, Matty Cash's deflected 87th-minute shot gives us a 1-0 third-round win at Middlesbrough – and progress to round four for the first time since 2016.

The draw pairs us with Chelsea at Stamford Bridge, where it finishes goalless after Douglas Luiz has an early effort ruled out by VAR for a handling offence.

In the league, a scrappy goalless encounter against Everton at Goodison Park is followed by Villa Park's only game of the month. Ollie Watkins scores his 15th league and cup goal of the season, but it's no more than a consolation in a 3-1 defeat by Newcastle – the first time Villa have lost at home in the Premier League for 11 months.

6th	MIDDLESBROUGH (FAC3) (A)	**1-0**	*Cash*
14th	EVERTON (A)	**0-0**	
26th	CHELSEA (FAC4) (A)	**0-0**	
30th	NEWCASTLE UNITED (H)	**1-3**	*Watkins*

FEBRUARY

A clinical display at Bramall Lane sees Villa romp to a 5-0 victory over Sheffield United. John McGinn opens the scoring before Ollie Watkins, Leon Bailey and Youri Tielemans extend the lead to 4-0 at the interval. Alex Moreno completes the scoring just after the interval.

Villa are also impressive at home to Manchester United, only for the visitors to grab a late winner after Douglas Luiz equalises with a well-taken goal. That disappointment is soon forgotten, though, as Watkins scores twice in a 2-1 victory over Fulham at Craven Cottage.

Luiz takes centre stage against Nottingham Forest at Villa Park, scoring twice to establish a 3-0 lead after Watkins opens the scoring. Although the visitors hit back with goals either side of half-time, Bailey grabs a fourth goal to secure three points.

3rd	SHEFFIELD UNITED (A)	5-0	McGinn, Watkins, Bailey, Tielemans, Moreno
7th	CHELSEA (FAC4 replay) (H)	1-3	Diaby
11th	MANCHESTER UNITED (H)	1-2	Luiz
17th	FULHAM (A)	2-1	Watkins 2
24th	NOTTINGHAM FOREST (H)	4-2	Watkins, Luiz 2, Bailey

MARCH

Leading 2-0 at half-time at Kenilworth Road, thanks to two well-taken Ollie Watkins goals, Villa almost let it slip as Luton Town storm back to draw level. But subs Moussa Diaby and Lucas Digne combine to grab a late winner, Digne heading home Diaby's cross at the far post.

Villa are badly out of sorts in a 4-0 home defeat by Tottenham Hotspur, a game in which John McGinn is sent off. Even so, they take a point from the next league fixture, substitute Nicolo Zaniolo's 79th-minute equaliser earning a 1-1 draw at West Ham – and the month ends on a high note.

Moussa Diaby's powerful shot and Ezri Konsa's dainty dink are enough to clinch a 2-0 home win in the derby against Wolves.

2nd	LUTON TOWN (A)	3-2	*Watkins 2, Digne*
7th	TOTTENHAM HOTSPUR (H)	0-4	
11th	WEST HAM (A)	1-1	*Zaniolo*
17th	WOLVES (H)	2-0	*Diaby, Konsa*

APRIL

After a heavy defeat at Manchester City, Villa lead 2-0 and trail 3-2 against Brentford at Villa Park. Ollie Watkins salvages a point with his second headed goal in the 80th minute, while Morgan Rogers is on target for the first time since his transfer from Middlesbrough.

Despite being without the suspended Douglas Luiz, Villa are 2-0 winners away to title contenders Arsenal. Late goals from Leon Bailey and Ollie Watkins make it a triumphant return to the Emirates for former Gunners' boss Unai Emery and goalkeeper Emi Martinez.

Villa trail at home to Bournemouth, but Rogers fires the equaliser before Moussa Diaby and Bailey complete two delightful second-half moves. That's followed by a 2-2 draw against Chelsea after Villa go two-up through a Marc Cucurella own goal, and Rogers' fine low shot.

3rd	MANCHESTER CITY (A)	1-4	*Duran*
6th	BRENTFORD (H)	3-3	*Watkins 2, Morgan*
14th	ARSENAL (A)	2-0	*Bailey, Watkins*
21st	BOURNEMOUTH (H)	3-1	*Rogers, Diaby, Bailey*
21st	CHELSEA (H)	2-2	*Cucurella og, Rogers*

MAY

As the race for fourth place hots up, both Villa and Tottenham Hotspur are starting to feel the pressure. Unai Emery's men suffer a 1-0 defeat to Brighton at the Amex Stadium but on the same afternoon, Spurs are beaten 4-2 at Liverpool.

Substitute Jhon Duran is the hero in a 3-3 thriller against Liverpool in the final home match, the Colombian striker netting two late goals to earn an important point after the visitors lead 3-1. Youri Tielemans had earlier driven home the equaliser after a rare slip from Emi Martinez had handed the visitors a second-minute opening goal.

Twenty-four hours later, Tottenham lose at home to champions-elect Manchester City, a result which secures fourth place for Villa and qualification for the UEFA Champions League.

Even a heavy defeat at Crystal Palace on the final day can't dampen the spirits of Villa supporters who celebrate their team's incredible season throughout the match at Selhurst Park.

5th	BRIGHTON & HA (A)	0-1	
13th	LIVERPOOL (H)	3-3	*Tielemans, Duran (2)*
19th	CRYSTAL PALACE (A)	0-5	

BACK ON THE EURO TRAIL

It ended in semi-final heartbreak, but Villa enjoyed a European adventure last season for the first time in 14 years.

Unai Emery's men qualified for the Europa Conference League by finishing seventh in 2022-23, and there were some memorable nights, both at Villa Park and on the continent.

The team also played a Scottish club for the first time in UEFA competition, overcoming Hibernian in the play-off round. A 5-0 first leg win in Edinburgh – including an Ollie Watkins hat-trick – equalled the club's biggest European success before the job was completed with a 3-0 home success.

After losing away to Legia Warsaw in the group stages, the team remained unbeaten in their subsequent games against HSK Zrinjski Mostar, AZ Alkmaar and Legia to finish top of Group E.

That ensured a direct passage to the round of 16, and a comfortable 4-0 victory over Ajax following a goalless draw in Amsterdam.

Both legs of the semi-final against Lille OSC ended in 2-1 home wins before Villa emerged 4-3 winners in a penalty shoot-out in France. Youri Tielemans,

Watkins, Matty Cash and Douglas Luiz converted their spot kicks and Emi Martinez made two saves.

The adventure ended against Olympiacos. Goals from Ollie Watkins and Moussa Diaby were not enough to prevent a 4-2 home defeat, and a 2-0 setback in Greece ended the dream of a place in the final.

PLAY-OFF			
Aug 23rd	HIBERNIAN	A	5-0
	Watkins 3, Bailey, Luiz (pen)		
Aug 31st	HIBERNIAN	H	3-0
	Duran, Bailey, Cash		

GROUP			
Sept 21st	LEGIA WARSZAWA	A	2-3
	Duran, Digne		
Oct 5th	HSK ZRINJSKI MOSTAR	H	1-0
	McGinn		
Oct 26th	AZ ALKMAAR	A	4-1
	Bailey, Tielemans, Watkins, McGinn		
Nov 9th	AZ ALKMAAR	H	2-1
	Carlos, Watkins		
Nov 30th	LEGIA WARSZAWA	H	2-1
	Diaby, Moreno		
Dec 14th	HSK ZRINJSKI MOSTAR	A	1-1
	Zaniolo		

ROUND OF 16			
Mar 7th	AJAX	A	0-0
Mar 14th	AJAX	H	4-0
	Watkins, Bailey, Duran, Diaby		

QUARTER-FINAL			
Apr 11th	LILLE OSC	H	2-1
	Watkins, McGinn		
Apr 18th	LILLE OSC	A	1-2

May 2nd	OLYMPIACOS	H	2-4
	Watkins, Diaby		
May 9th	OLYMPIACOS	A	0-2

OFF THE MARK

TEN PLAYERS SCORED THEIR FIRST VILLA GOALS LAST SEASON...

JHON DURAN
v Everton (h) **4-0**

The Colombian youngster capitalises on a mix-up in the visitors' defence to race through and calmly slot a low left-foot shot past Jordan Pickford.

PAU TORRES
v Wolves (a) **1-1**

Two minutes after Wolves take the lead at Molineux, the Spanish centre-back converts an Ollie Watkins cross with a left-foot shot from six yards.

MOUSSA DIABY
v Newcastle United (a) **1-5**

Lucas Digne's cross from the left is headed on by Ollie Watkins, and the French midfielder marks his debut with a perfect right foot half-volley.

BOUBACAR KAMARA
v Everton (h) **1-2**

The midfielder fires home right-footed from just outside the penalty in a League Cup tie after a Douglas Luiz corner is headed clear.

YOURI TIELEMANS
v AZ Alkmaar (a) **4-1**

Controlling a pass from John McGinn, the Belgian midfielder sends a low shot through the keeper's legs in Villa's third group Europa Conference League game.

ALEX MORENO
v Legia Warszawa (h) **2-1**

A close-range volley, following a Douglas Luiz free-kick clinches victory over the Poles after Moussa Diaby's early strike is nullified by a Legia equaliser.

DIEGO CARLOS
v AZ Alkmaar (h) **2-1**

The Brazilian centre-back climbs to meet a Leon Bailey corner with a header to put Villa level after the Dutch side take the lead.

NICOLO ZANIOLO
v HSK Zrinjsky (a) **1-1**

The Italy international controls a left-wing cross from John McGinn and calmly strokes the ball home from close range.

LEANDER DENDONCKER
v Manchester United (a) **2-3**

A neat, close-range flick puts Villa two-up at Old Trafford after Clement Lenglet heads down John McGinn's corner.

MORGAN ROGERS
v Brentford (h) **3-3**

Less than a minute after the interval, Rogers moves into a pass from Youri Tielemans and cuts inside to send a low left-foot shot inside the near post.

EURO RIVALS

European football is back on the Villa agenda, and our ECL quarter-final first leg against Lille OSC was the club's 100th game in UEFA competition. We have hidden the names of 12 teams Villa have faced over the years in the grid below.

Answers on page 60.

B	A	R	C	E	L	O	N	A	J
D	L	C	S	K	A	R	U	N	K
E	K	Z	L	A	L	E	N	D	V
P	M	Q	T	O	I	N	T	E	R
O	A	J	A	X	L	N	B	R	W
R	A	T	K	N	L	E	D	L	H
T	R	C	E	P	E	S	T	E	M
I	F	A	T	L	E	T	I	C	O
V	A	L	U	R	G	M	D	H	F
O	D	B	A	S	E	L	F	T	K

ALKMAAR		CSKA	
ANDERLECHT		DEPORTIVO	
AJAX		LILLE	
ATLETICO		HF	
BARCELONA		RENNES	
BASEL		VALUR	

ARE YOU AN AV STUDENT?

It's exam time, but don't worry – all the questions are about Aston Villa! Here's a chance to display your knowledge of all things claret and blue... **Answers on page 61.**

HISTORY

1. Villa's last FA Cup triumph was against Manchester United at Wembley. In which year did it happen?

2. Which player scored both goals in Villa's 2-1 win that day?

3. When did Villa last win the League Championship?

4. Who is the club's highest scorer in the Premier League?

5. Villa faced the same opponent in each of their first three FA Cup finals. Which team was it?

GEOGRAPHY

1. Villa have played over 100 games in European competitions. Who were our opponents in the club's first UEFA Cup tie in 1975?

2. The club's 100th UEFA game was last season's quarter-final. Who were our opponents?

3. In which Scottish city was John McGinn born?

4. Which Spanish club did Villa face in both the UEFA Cup in 1978 and the UEFA Super Cup in 1983?

5. In which Japanese city did Villa face South American champions Penarol in the 1982 World Clubs Championship?

MATHS

1. Ollie Watkins was Villa's leading Premier League marksman last season. How many league goals did he score?

2. Villa scored a total of 76 goals in the Premier League last season, and conceded 61. What was the team's goal difference?

3. Using the 2023-24 squad numbers, what do you get if you add Emi Martinez, John McGinn and Leon Bailey?

4. Villa recorded their highest aggregate success in a European tie in last season's ECL games against Hibernian. Can you recall how many they scored over the two legs?

5. Villa's points total last season was their highest for a 38-game Premier League season. Can you recall what it was?

CURRENT AFFAIRS

1. Villa are playing this season in the UEFA Champions League. What was the competition's original name?

2. Which Hollywood superstar was a guest at the ECL semi-final against Olympiacos at Villa Park?

3. Jhon Duran is only the second Colombian to play for Villa. Who was the first?

4. Which three counties did Villa visit for pre-season games this summer?

5. Who was Villa's player-of-the-year for 2023-24?

THE NUMBERS GAME

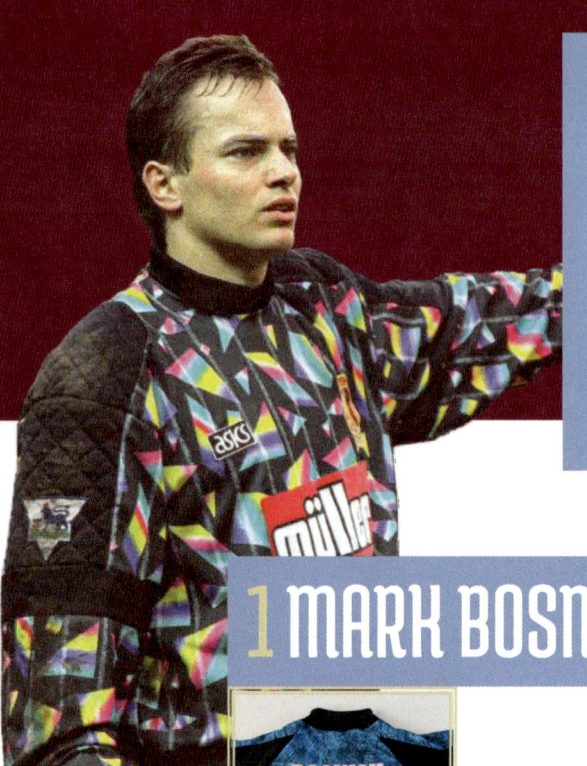

Squad numbers now have no limit, and Omari Kellyman wore number 71 when he broke in Villa's first team last season.

But there was a time when players wore numbers 1 to 11 in every match. Here's a Villa team of Villa stars, based on their numbers. These, plus many other match-worn Villa shirts, can be viewed at Dave Hitchman's impressive website: **www.astonvillashirts.co.uk**

1 MARK BOSNICH

2 KENNY SWAIN

3 DIEGO CARLOS

4 OLAF MELLBERG

5 PAUL MCGRATH

7 IAN TAYLOR

8 BRIAN LITTLE

6 DENNIS MORTIMER

9 ALAN MCINALLY

10 JOHN CAREW

11 GABBY AGBONLAHOR

47

OLLIE WATKINS

DOING YOUR HOMEWORK!

Homework is an essential (if sometimes unpopular!) aspect of education. And it is equally important in modern-day football.

When it comes to recruiting new players, Villa's backroom staff always thoroughly research any potential new signings.

Aussie goalkeeper Joe Gauci discovered as much when he joined the club from Adelaide United on the 2024 transfer deadline day.

"The level of detail they went into about my game was amazing," he said. "You could tell how much they had analysed me as a goalkeeper, and as a person as well.

"The areas they went into about how I can improve were really detailed. I feel I can take my game to another level.

"This is a big step up from Australian football but it's something I'm looking forward to."

Joe is the second Australian goalkeeper to sign for Villa. The first was Mark Bosnich, who played 228 games between 1991 and 1999, when he moved to Manchester United.

KOSTA KILO!

He was on the pitch for just 15 minutes – including eight minutes of added time – but Kosta Nedeljkovic created a piece of Villa history on the opening day of the 2024-25 campaign.

When the Serbian teenager went on as a substitute for Matty Cash in the 2-1 win at West Ham, he became the club's 1,000th first-team player.

Villa's Legacy Numbers initiative had been launched just a few days earlier. Starting with the team's first FA Cup tie in 1879, every player who had played an official game was listed in order of appearance.

Amadou Onana, who marked his debut by scoring after just four minutes, became Villan 998, while Dutch defender Ian Maatsen was 999 when he replaced Lucas Digne on 74 minutes.

Then came the late change which made Nedeljkovic the landmark 1,000. That number, of course, is frequently written as 1K, based on the Greek word kilo, which means one thousand.

So, if you find the former Red Star Belgrade player's surname too difficult to pronounce, just call him Kosta Kilo!

WHICH CLUB DID I SIGN FROM?

Can you match up these Villa players with the clubs from which they signed?

To get you started, the answer to No.1 PAU TORRES is B VILLAREAL

Answers on page 60.

 PAU **TORRES** 1

 TYRONE **MINGS** 2

 JOHN **MCGINN** 3

 YOURI **TIELEMANS** 4

 BOUBACAR **KAMARA** 5

 EMI **MARTINEZ** 6

 EMI **BUENDIA** 7

EZRI **KONSA** 8

A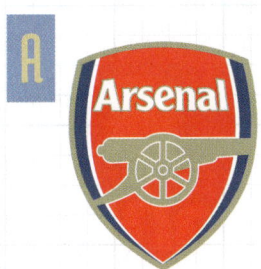

B

C

D

E

F

G

H

JACOB RAMSEY

SPOT THE DIFFERENCE

These photos look identical at the first glance but there are six differences. Can you spot them?

Answers on page 61.

A CENTURY AND A HALF OF MEMORIES

The year 2025 marks the 150th anniversary of Villa's first matches. Although the club was founded towards the end of 1874, bad weather that winter meant that they were unable to play until early in the new year. Villa's special anniversary is being celebrated by the club throughout the 2024-25 season, with various events organised by the AV150 board.

Here are a few quirky facts with which to impress your pals!

THE FIRST GAME

Many people believe that the club's first fixture was against Aston Brook St Mary's in March 1875, a half-and-half match of rugby in the first half and football in the second. But Villa actually played two months earlier, on Saturday 9th January, a 14-a-side match against Aston Park Unity. A report in the Birmingham Daily Mail recorded that it was a well-contested match, which was won by the Unity team. The teams met again that month, Unity winning again. But Villa finally managed their first win when John Hughes scored the only goal against St Mary's in a rugby/football match in March.

UNKNOWN RECORD

Archie Hunter is Villa's record FA Cup scorer – although we don't know exactly how many he scored. Hunter, a skilful Scot who was the club's first superstar, scored at least 34 goals in Cup ties. And he was probably also on target at least once in a 5-3 victory over Wednesbury Strollers in 1880. Unfortunately we can't be sure – because the scorers were not published in any newspaper or magazine.

HERO AND VILLAIN

Chris Nicholl scored all four goals at Filbert Street in March 1976. Unfortunately, two of them into Villa's net! The central defender twice gave Leicester City the lead with own goals. But he made amends with equalisers which earned a 2-2 draw.

COMEBACK COWANS

Gordon Cowans is the only player to have had THREE separate spells as a Villa player. The classy midfielder, who made his debut in 1976, was a member of the League Championship and European Cup-winning team in the early 1980s. After three years with Italian club Bari, he returned in 1988 – and again in 1993 following a spell with Blackburn Rovers.

DEADLY DALIAN

Dalian Atkinson scored Villa's first goal in the new FA Premier League in August 1992. The striker's late equaliser earned a 1-1 draw against Ipswich Town at Portman Road. Atkinson in fact scored in each of the club's first three Premier League matches. He was also on target in 1-1 draws at home to Leeds United and Southampton.

THE 20,000 MARC

Marc Albrighton had the distinction of scoring the Premier League's 20,000th goal when he netted against Arsenal in December 2011. Sadly, his goal wasn't enough to prevent a 2-1 home defeat, but it earned the winger a £20,000 charity cheque, which he donated to Acorns Children's Hospice.

OLLIE ON FIRE

Ollie Watkins' 19-goal league haul last season made him Villa's highest Premier League scorer in a single season. The last time a player scored more was in 1980-81, when Peter Withe's 20 goals helped to clinch the League Championship.

365 DAY MEMBERSHIP

BECOME PART OF THE VILLA

Our junior fans can get access to some fantastic benefits, including:

- Priority ticket access
- 10% Soccer school discount*
- 10% off Stadium Tour
- Exclusive members events
- Birthday and Christmas card
- Exclusive competitions
- Member only content
- Match Predictor competition
- Games and downloads
- Plus much, much more...

Villans
(12-17)

Cubs
(3-11)

Little Villans
(0-2)

TO LEARN MORE VISIT **MEMBERSHIP.AVFC.CO.UK**

*Age restrictions apply

VILLA||MEMBERSHIPS

SPOT THE BALL

There are eight match balls in this pic of Emi Martinez
saving a shot against Arsenal, but only one of
them is real. Can you spot which one it is?

Answers found on page 61.

THE DEBUT LINE-UP!

Villa could have fielded a team of new boys last season, with 11 players making their debuts – six new signings plus five Academy graduates.

FILIP MARSCHALL
Zrinjski Mostar (a)

FINLEY MUNROE
v Olympiacos (a)

CLEMENT LENGLET,
v Legia Warszawa (a)

PAU TORRES
v Newcastle United (a)

SEB REVAN
v Hibernian (h)

YOURI TIELEMANS
v Newcastle United (a)

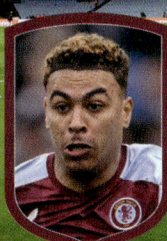

MORGAN ROGERS
v Sheffield United (a))

TOMMI O'REILLY
v Zrinjski Mostar (a))

NICOLO ZANIOLO
v Burnley (a)

OMARI KELLYMAN
v Hibernian (h)

MOUSSA DIABY
v Newcastle United (a)

ANSWERS

WHICH IS MY SHIRT?

1.	TORRES	7.	MARTINEZ
2.	TIELEMANS	8.	WATKINS
3.	MORENO	9.	CARLOS
4.	KAMARA	10.	ROGERS
5.	BARKLEY	11.	RAMSEY
6.	KONSA	12.	DURAN

FACT OR FIB

1. FACT
2. FIB (Christian Benteke also scored two Premier League hat-tricks for Villa)
3. FIB (Youri Tielemans signed from Leicester City)
4. FACT
5. FACT
6. FIB (Ollie Watkins provided the most assists)
7. FACT
8. FIB (Villa finished second in 1992-93)
9. FACT
10. FIB (It was Tom HANKS, who is an avid Villa fan!)

DO YOU KNOW EMI MARTINEZ?

1. A, ARSENAL
2. C, ARGENTINA
3. B, SHEFFIELD UNITED
4. C, LILLE OSC
5. B, MAR DEL PLATA

EURO RIVALS

B	A	R	C	E	L	O	N	A	J
D	L	C	S	K	A	R	U	N	K
E	K	Z	L	A	L	E	N	D	V
P	M	Q	T	O	I	N	T	E	R
O	A	J	A	X	L	N	B	R	W
R	A	T	K	N	L	E	D	L	H
T	R	C	E	P	E	S	T	E	M
I	F	A	T	L	E	T	I	C	O
V	A	L	U	R	G	M	D	H	F
O	D	B	A	S	E	L	F	T	K

WHICH CLUB DID I SIGN FROM?

1. PAU TORRES – B, VILLAREAL
2. TYRONE MINGS – E, BOURNEMOUTH
3. JOHN McGINN – D, HIBERNIAN
4. YOURI TIELEMANS – G, LEICESTER CITY
5. BOUBACAR KAMARA – H, MARSEILLE
6. EMI MARTINEZ – A, ARSENAL
7. EMI BUENDIA – F, NORWICH CITY
8. EZRI KONSA – C, BRENTFORD

SPOT THE DIFFERENCE

SPOT THE BALL

ARE YOU AN AV STUDENT?

HISTORY
1. 1957
2. Peter McParland
3. 1980-81
4. Gabby Agbonlahor
5. West Bromwich Albion (1887, 1892, 1895)

GEOGRAPHY
1. Royal Antwerp
2. Lille OSC
3. Glasgow
4. Barcelona
5. Tokyo

MATHS
1. 19
2. +15
3. 39
4. Eight
5 68 points

CURRENT AFFAIRS
1. The European Cup
2. Actor Tom Hanks
3. Juan Pablo Angel
4. USA, Slovakia and Germany
5. Ollie Watkins.